A Small Christmas

by Wong Herbert Yee

Houghton Mifflin Company
Boston

www.houghtonmifflinbooks.com

The text of this book is set in 16-point Apollo MT.
The illustrations are watercolor.

Library of Congress Cataloging-in-Publication Data

Yee, Wong Herbert.
A Small Christmas / by Wong Herbert Yee.
p. cm.
Summary: After finding a Christmas tree for Mayor
Mole, Fireman Small has a busy Christmas Eve
as he fills in for Santa Claus.
HC ISBN-13: 978-0-618-32612-9
PB ISBN-13: 978-0-618-91534-7
[1. Christmas—Fiction. 2. Fire fighters—Fiction.
3. Santa Claus—Fiction. 4. Animals—Fiction.
5. Stories in rhyme.] I. Title.
PZ8.3.Y42Sm 2004
[E]—dc22
2003017467

Printed in Malaysia
TWP 10 9 8 7 6 5 4 3 2

To Judy, with love

In the middle of town, where buildings stand tall,
There lives a little man called Fireman Small.
The only fireman this side of the bay
Is getting ready for the holiday!
Since no calls have come in, he's also free
To help Mayor Mole find a Christmas tree.

On Beaver's Tree Farm, they grow pines big and tall
And some *teeny-tiny*, like Fireman Small.
With a few mighty WHACKS! he chops a tree down,
Throws it on the truck, and drives back to town.

The city is bustling with yuletide cheer.

For stores it's the busiest time of the year.

Fireman Small waves to a holiday shopper

As he straightens the Christmas tree topper.

There are bundles of lights that need to get strung,

Boxes of ornaments waiting to be hung.

The townsfolk hustle past Small on the street.

Some stop to sample a warm winter treat.

Boys and girls climb onto Santa's lap.

Moms and dads line up with presents to wrap.

Soon it's time for shopkeepers to leave,
Since stores all close early on Christmas Eve.
Fireman Small puts up the last decoration.
Tired and beat, he drives back to the station.

He pulls the truck into firehouse nine,
Walks upstairs one step at a time.
Closes the curtains, gets in bed,
And pulls the covers over his head.

Around midnight, he hears a sound on the roof,

A jingling of sleigh bells, the *tip-tap* of hoof.

There's a CRASH! . . . then a muffled *ho-ho-ho*.

Someone's downstairs in the firehouse below!

Quickly out of bed he scoots,
Jumps into his pants and boots.
Ready to go, he slides down the pole,
Sees two legs sticking out of the coal!

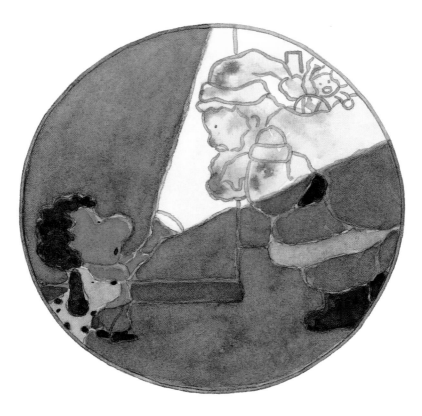

Black boots, a brown sack, white bearded jaws . . .

Is it a burglar? Why—it's Santa Claus!

From the cap on his head right down to each foot,

The jolly old fellow is covered in soot!

His clothes get tossed in the washing machine.
In just a short while, they're dry and clean!
Uh-oh! Something's wrong. The red suit has *shrunk!*

Worse than that, Santa's asleep in his bunk!

What about all the good girls and boys?

Who will deliver the rest of the toys?

Though Fireman Small should be snuggled in bed,

He races up to the rooftop instead.

Dressed in Santa's suit, he hops in the sleigh.

But the reindeer refuse to fly away!

What can he do now? Such *terrible* luck!
Wait! Fireman Small can take the fire truck!
Out of the station, he's ready to go,
Plowing through streets all covered with snow.
Fireman Small clutches the sack full of toys.
He slides down the chimney without any noise.

At Farmer Pig's farm, he leaves a straw hat,
New overalls, and a chew toy for Cat.
Beaver's gift is her own Ping-Pong paddle.
Rabbit gets a rocking horse and a saddle.

Up the chimney he scoots in a hurry.

Down the rooftop he shoots with a flurry.

Fireman Small speeds along to the next house,
Dropping off presents for Possum and Mouse.

He stuffs a stocking for Crocodile's daughter.
Makes sure the Christmas tree has enough water.
Fireman Small crosses each name off his list.
The bag is empty. No one has been missed.

He pulls back into station number nine.

Walks upstairs, one step at a time.

Stretches and yawns, crawls into bed . . .

And pulls the covers over his head.

When Fireman Small gets up on Christmas Day,

He finds no Santa, no reindeer or sleigh.

Was it a dream? Did he imagine it all?

Look! There's a letter for Fireman Small:

After flying all night,
North, south, east, and west,
My reindeer and I
Were in need of some rest.
Thank you, Fireman Small,
You're a fine substitute.
Please keep this token,
My now tiny red suit!